Copyright © 2004 by Nord-Süd Verlag AG, Gossau Zürich, Switzerland
First published in Switzerland under the title *Das Geschenk fürs Christkind.*
English translation copyright © 2004 by North-South Books Inc., New York

All rights reserved. No part of this book may be reproduced or utilized in any form
or by any means, electronic or mechanical, including photocopying, recording, or any
information storage and retrieval system, without permission in writing from the publisher.

First published in the United States, Great Britain, Canada, Australia, and New Zealand in 2004
by North-South Books, an imprint of Nord-Süd Verlag AG, Gossau Zürich, Switzerland.
Distributed in the United States by North-South Books Inc., New York.

Library of Congress Cataloging-in-Publication Data is available.
A CIP catalogue record for this book is available from The British Library.
ISBN 0-7358-1957-2 (trade edition)
1 3 5 7 9 HC 10 8 6 4 2
ISBN 0-7358-1958-0 (library edition)
1 3 5 7 9 LE 10 8 6 4 2
Printed in Belgium

For more information about our books, and the authors and artists
who create them, visit our web site: www.northsouth.com

Tina Jähnert

A Gift for the Christ Child

ILLUSTRATED BY

Alessandra Roberti

Translated by Sibylle Kazeroid

North-South Books

New York | London

Miriam had a wish. She wished with all her heart that she was bigger, more important.

Her older brother, Malachai, was very, very important. He was allowed to do things around the inn that Miriam could only dream about. She was always told, "Miriam, don't do that; you're too little."

It was a busy time at the inn. For weeks, people had been coming to Bethlehem to sign the registers because everyone—*everyone*—was going to be counted.

And because of this there was more to do than ever. Mother cooked, Father served, and Malachai went to the market by himself every morning to buy vegetables, to bargain, and to gossip.

Only Miriam, the smallest, was always left out.

One day she had enough.

Armed with her red blanket to protect and comfort her, she bravely climbed into her mother's lap.

"Mother, I want to help, too, and be important!"

"Miriam, my sweet child, you are too small to cook or carry water," said Mother. "But believe me, you are important, to me and to everyone who knows you. Just because you are you—unique in the whole world. But since you want so much to help, from now on, I'll try to find things that you can do."

Miriam nodded. "Good! I'll go and play now, until you need me."

Happily, Miriam played with the
little lamb and with Hannah, her doll.
She clowned around with Malachai,
until a group of new guests arrived
and he had to help.

So many strangers were in their inn now.

They ran in, they ran out. They made a huge racket.

They were so noisy that Miriam almost didn't hear when her mother called, "Miriam! Miriam, can you help me, please?"

Miriam raced through the kitchen to the backyard.

"What can I do?" she asked her mother, out of breath.

Then she saw that her mother was not alone. With her were a man and a young woman on a donkey.

"Miriam, could you please lead these two guests down to the stable?" asked Mother. "The inn is full. I don't have a single room left. Be careful that the little donkey doesn't slip on the smooth stones."

Miriam took her job very seriously. She knew it was important to find the safest path to the stable. Slowly, very slowly, she led the way down the hill.

Miriam didn't think that the young woman would
be happy in the stable. So she was very surprised when
the woman thanked God in heaven for the quiet and
the fresh straw. She thanked Him for the animals and
the little lamb. That made Miriam very happy.

Much too quickly, Malachai came looking for Miriam. "Time for bed," he said.

"Good night," the young woman called softly.

Miriam was very tired. It had been a long day.

Father gave her a big kiss, and Mother tucked her in.

Miriam hugged her blanket tightly and murmured her nightly prayers. Soon she was fast asleep.

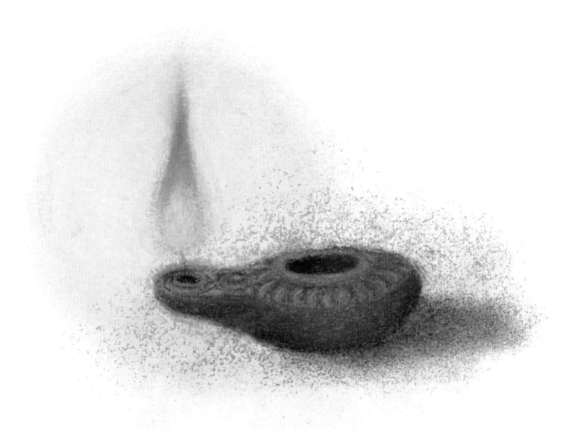

Suddenly, in the middle of the silent night, Miriam woke.

There was a light shining in the stable. How strange. Maybe the couple needed something.

Quickly Miriam wrapped her warm blanket around her and hurried out.

Miriam crept quietly into the stable. There, sitting in the hay, was the young woman. She held a newborn baby in her arms and looked very happy.

Miriam knew just what to do.

She took the warm blanket from her shoulders, folded it, then carefully laid it in the straw-filled manger.

"I would like to give this to the little baby," she said.

Miriam's heart leaped with joy when she saw the young mother gently wrap the baby in Miriam's blanket.

There was a knock at the door. Outside stood shepherds. They spoke excitedly of angels who had told them that Jesus Christ, the son of God, had been born to save the world.

Miriam listened spellbound. Soon Mother, Father, and Malachai were there, too. In awe, they all approached the manger. Full of joy and thanks, they praised God.

Mother pointed to the red blanket. She smiled at Miriam and said, "That was a very sweet thing to do."

Miriam felt big and tall and proud. She finally knew that she *was* important, not just to Mother, but also to the Child in the manger, and so to the whole wide world.